There was an
old woman
who lived
in a
shoe

Kate Toms

make
believe
ideas

There was an **old woman** who lived in a shoe,

with so many *children* —

what could they all do?

Every day, they had some fun,

but not until

the **chores** were done!

On **Monday,** they have clothes to wash,

and sheets to **clean**

with a **splish** and a **splosh.**

Spinning around in the **big** machine, the laundry is soon all **fresh** and clean.

soapso

Now watch them **pull** with all their might —

they've tied the laundry to their **kite!**

There was an **old woman**
who lived in a shoe,
with so many **children**
and **so much** to do.

On **Tuesday,** every child must choose
some polish and a pair of shoes.
They **scrape** and **brush** and **polish** hard,
in a **line** out in the yard.

Later on, they go for a **swim**,

put armbands on, and **JUMP** right in!

They **laugh** and **dive**

and **splash about**

and towels are **ready**
when they get out.

There was an **old woman** who lived in a **shoe**,
with so many **children** — how the time **flew!**

On **Wednesday,** they get on their knees
to pick some carrots, beans, and peas —
there's lots of digging, gathering **berries,**
and filling bowls with piles of **cherries!**
Then ...

it's **music time** for girls and boys,

lots of singing, lots of **noise!**

They **dance** and **sing** and twirl around

and make a really **amazing** sound.

On **Thursday,** a trip to the vet's

Once they are **home,** they brush the **fur.**

food

to get a **checkup** for the **pets**.

Listen to the kittens **purrr!**

milk

On **Friday**, it's off to the **park** to play –

a **happy** way to spend the day.

A **picnic's** packed, the stroller's full –
and don't forget
the **bouncy** ball!

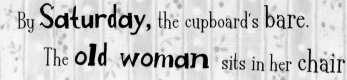

By **Saturday,** the cupboard's bare.
The **old woman** sits in her chair

to make a **list** of things they need,
with so many **hungry** mouths to feed!

A **shopping** trip
is quickly planned,
and everybody
lends a hand.

Soon the **cart** is piled high with all the things they need to **buy.**

Sunday is the day of rest –

see them in their

Sunday best,